The Circus Elephant

Come meet the Star!!!   James Elephant!!!

By: Nicki Snyder

Copyright © 2004 Nicki Snyder
First published by AuthorHouse 07/2004

2nd Edition Copyright © 2017

ISBN: 1544695624
ISBN-13: 978-1544695624

To my mother:
Thank you for staying up late with me while I finished this book.

This is the circus.

James Elephant is the star.
Everyone knows and loves James.

James likes to do neat tricks,
like juggling balls and twirling a hula-hoop,
while balancing on a ball.

Soon there is a new circus animal.
His name is Tommy Seal.

Tommy becomes the new star.
He does better tricks than James.

James gets very sad. He decides to leave.

James Elephant is in his room looking in the newspaper.
He is studying the ads.

He packs up his things
and goes to look for a new job.

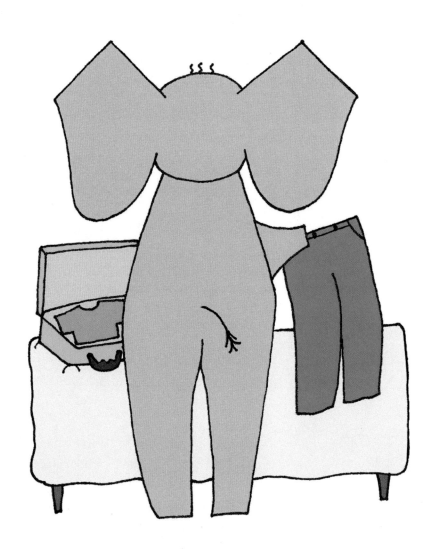

Meanwhile at the circus,
people are starting to miss James.
Some of the circus animals want to go look for him.

All of the circus performers take the day off to go look for their lost elephant.

James has been trying out job after job,
and either the job is too hard,
or James doesn't like it.

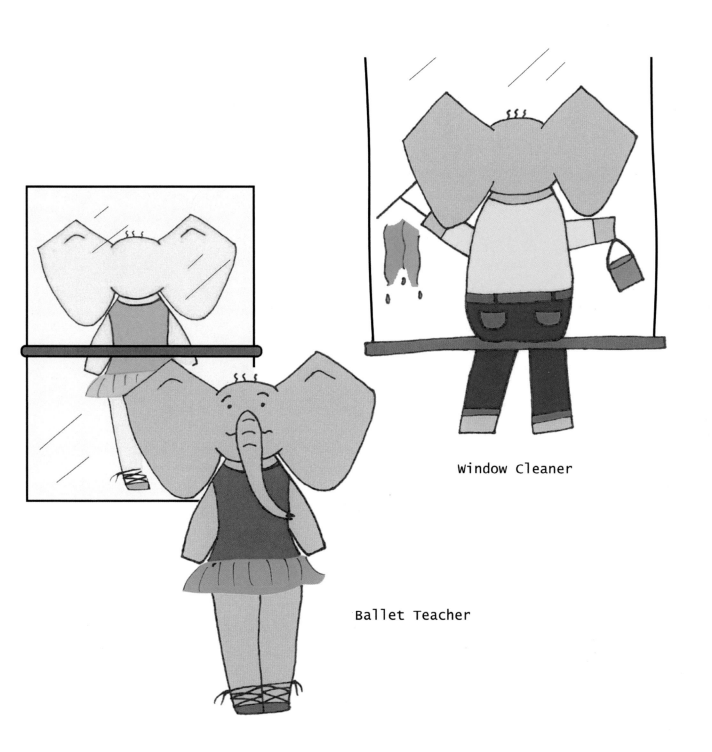

Window Cleaner

Ballet Teacher

James starts missing his friends and decides to go look for them.

Without knowing it,
James keeps passing his circus friends.
Tommy, who isn't watching where he is going,
falls into the sewer.
The performers rush to get help for poor Tommy.

It is starting to get dark and
James is getting lonely, so he heads home.

On his way home, he falls into the sewer,
and lands with a loud "thump".

James looks at the water
and see an alligator chasing Tommy Seal!

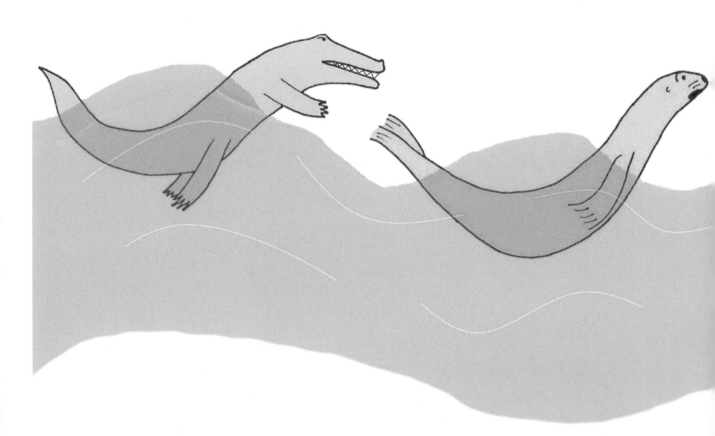

James takes his trunk, reaches in
and pulls Tommy to safety.

James climbs the steps to the street.
Circus members and people are there cheering.

Later, when they arrive at the circus,
Tommy and the performers ask James if
he wants his job back for saving Tommy.
James decides to accept.

James becomes famous again,
and learns to share the spotlight.
Now everyone in the circus is happy!

About the author:

Nicki was born in Texas on a military base.
She has lived many places, including Italy,
where she wrote this book as a school project.

The Circus Elephant is the first book
Nicki had published.

Made in the USA
Middletown, DE
15 September 2022

10550458R00015